Tudor Tales William at Hampton Court

by Alan Wybrow

Tudor Tales William at Hampton Court

First published in 2015
MadeGlobal Publishing
Text © 2015 Alan Wybrow
All Illustrations © 2015 Alan Wybrow

ISBN: 978-84-943721-7-9

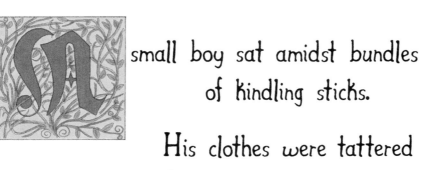 small boy sat amidst bundles of kindling sticks.

His clothes were tattered and worn, his feet bare and bruised, his face dirty and smudged, and his eyes tired and lonely.

He was a sad little street orphan named William.

Early each morning, he went to the surrounding forest and gathered kindling sticks. He sold them on the streets of London for a few farthings.

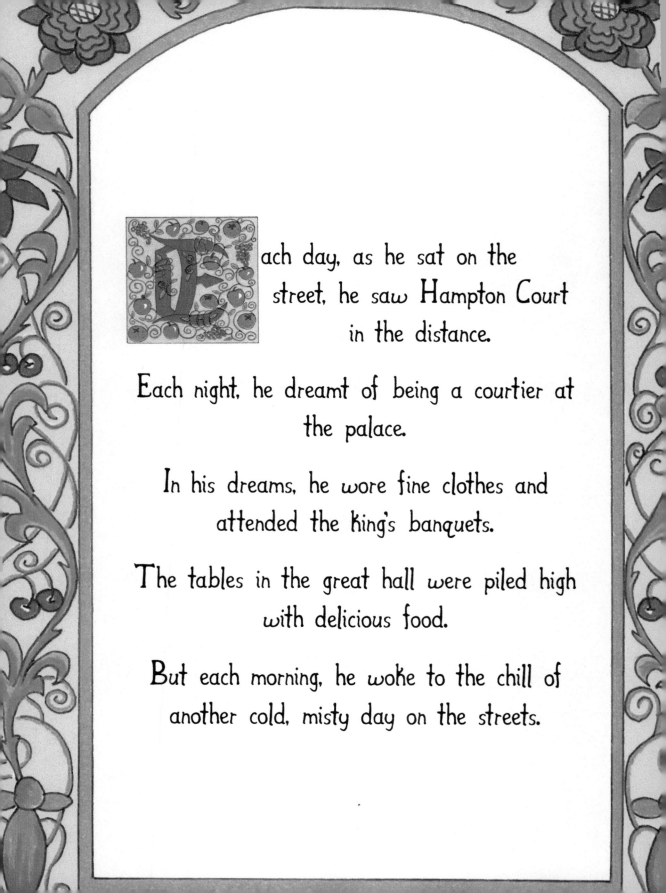

Each day, as he sat on the street, he saw Hampton Court in the distance.

Each night, he dreamt of being a courtier at the palace.

In his dreams, he wore fine clothes and attended the king's banquets.

The tables in the great hall were piled high with delicious food.

But each morning, he woke to the chill of another cold, misty day on the streets.

ne day, a stranger happened by. He stopped and asked William,

"What is the price of your kindling sticks, lad?"

William looked up at the stranger and replied, "A penny or two, sire. Whatever you can spare."

"What do you do with your earnings?" continued the stranger.

"I buy food to eat, sire," replied William.

"Where do you live and where is your family?" asked the stranger.

I have no family, sire, and I live wherever is found a warm, safe place," replied William.

he stranger was a kind man and felt sorry for William.

William reminded him of his own small son who had died a few years back.

The stranger asked, "What do they call you, lad?"

"I am called William, sire," was the reply.

William asked, "Who are you, sire?"

"I am Edmund, master cook in King Henry VIII's kitchens at Hampton Court," replied the stranger.

"Would you be interested in working for me, William?" asked Edmund, "I have need of a strong lad in the kitchens as a spit boy."

"A spit boy, sire?" a confused
William asked.

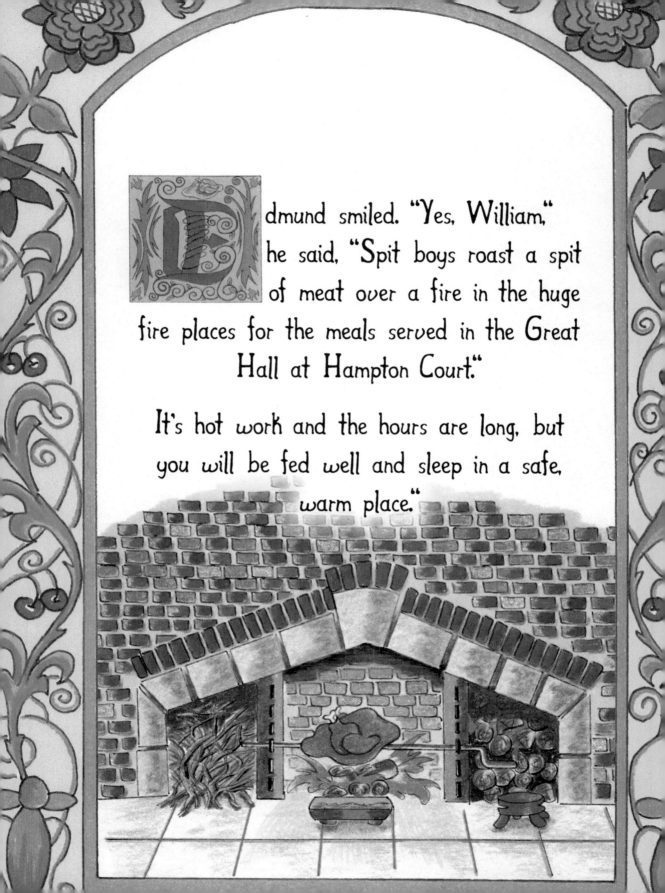

dmund smiled. "Yes, William," he said, "Spit boys roast a spit of meat over a fire in the huge fire places for the meals served in the Great Hall at Hampton Court."

It's hot work and the hours are long, but you will be fed well and sleep in a safe, warm place."

Food to eat and a warm place to sleep appealed to little William.

He agreed and set off with Edmund to Hampton Court.

dmund was very kind to William and taught him to be the best spit boy at Hampton Court.

One day, Edmund told William he would be accompanying the kitchen staff on the King's hunting trip.

William was excited!

He would get away from the hot kitchens of Hampton Court for a while, and into the fresh air of the English countryside!

On the trip, William travelled with the supply carts at the rear of the procession.

He saw the king riding in front, looking proud and magnificent on his trusty steed.

illiam spent his time roasting meat from the day's hunt.

He helped Edmund serve meals placed on long tables inside a large tent.

There was more food than William had ever seen before, and he thought about the dreams he used to have when he was living on the street.

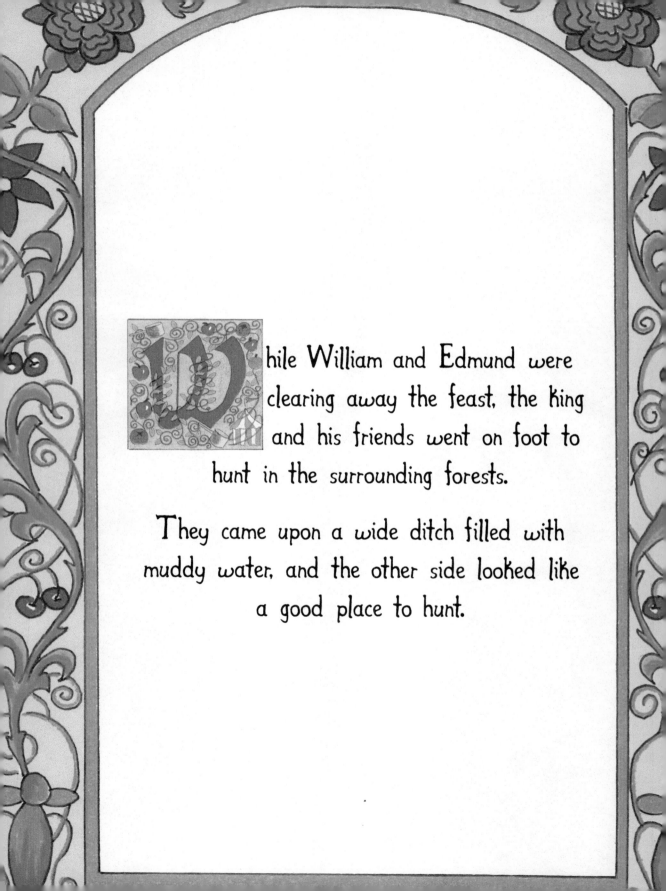

While William and Edmund were clearing away the feast, the king and his friends went on foot to hunt in the surrounding forests.

They came upon a wide ditch filled with muddy water, and the other side looked like a good place to hunt.

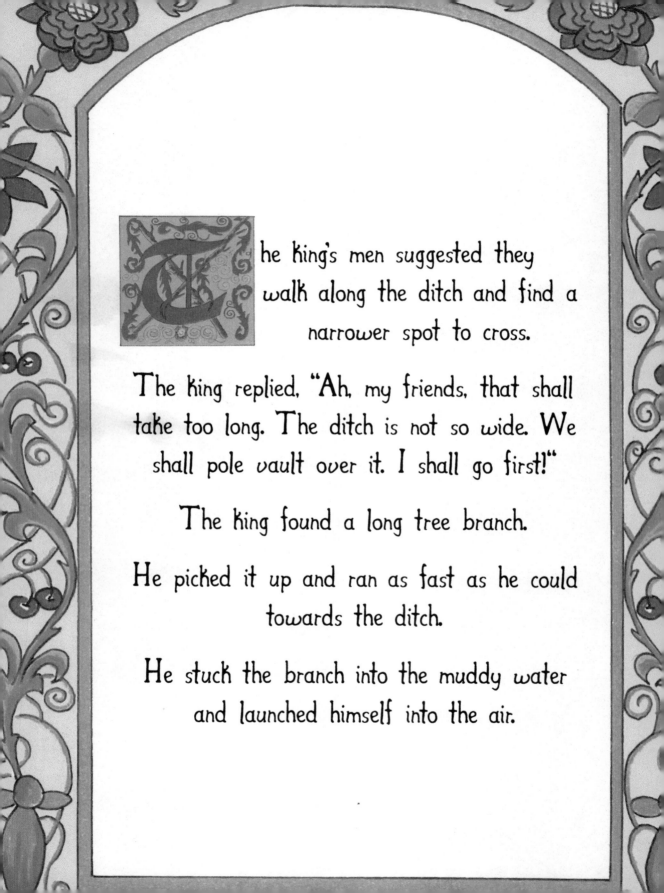

The king's men suggested they walk along the ditch and find a narrower spot to cross.

The king replied, "Ah, my friends, that shall take too long. The ditch is not so wide. We shall pole vault over it. I shall go first!"

The king found a long tree branch.

He picked it up and ran as fast as he could towards the ditch.

He stuck the branch into the muddy water and launched himself into the air.

uddenly, there was a loud CRACK!

The branch snapped and down went the king.

SPLOOSH!

He fell head first into the muddy water!

The king's head and face were stuck in the mud.

He struggled to free himself but the mud held fast.

His friends pulled and pulled on his legs.

That didn't work.

King Henry was stuck!

enry had to be dug out,
but how?

They did not have a shovel!

HELP! HELP!

His friends shouted.

William was cleaning a pot when he heard their cries for help.

He immediately ran towards the ditch, clinging onto the pot.

I'm coming!

William saw the king stuck in the mud.

He used the pot as a shovel and quickly freed the king's head from the mud.

The king sat up.

His face had turned blue.

He wiped mud from his eyes and saw William standing in front of him.

William was holding onto a very muddy pot.

he king's men cheered!

"Are you the one who rescued me from that wretched mud?" spluttered the king.

"Yes, Your Majesty," replied William.

"Who are you?" asked the king.

"My name is William, Your Majesty. I am a spit boy in your kitchens at Hampton Court," replied William.

The king paused, looked at William for a moment, and then commanded a guard to hand him a sword.

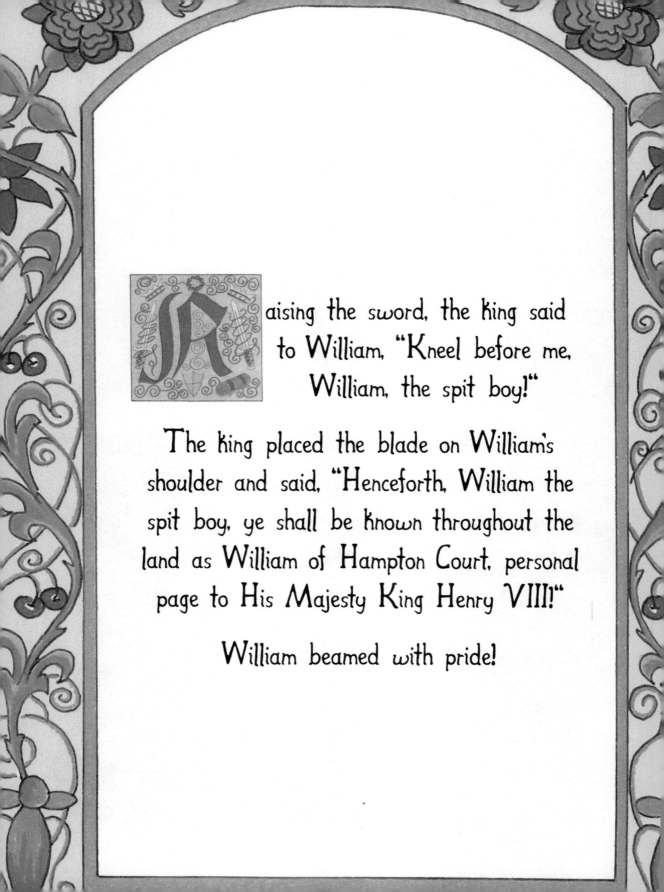

aising the sword, the king said to William, "Kneel before me, William, the spit boy!"

The king placed the blade on William's shoulder and said, "Henceforth, William the spit boy, ye shall be known throughout the land as William of Hampton Court, personal page to His Majesty King Henry VIII!"

William beamed with pride!

s the cheers echoed back to camp, Edmund smiled proudly.

A tear of joy trickled down his cheek as he said softly, "Cheers to my lad, William of Hampton Court!"

Well done William!

Historical Note

This fun story is based on a real historical event, although William is a fictional character. Tudor chronicler Edward Hall records what happened to the King Henry VIII in 1525 while he was out hawking near Hitchin in Hertfordshire.

"In this year, the king following his hawk leapt over a ditch beside Hitchin, with a pole and the pole broke, so that if one Edmund Mody, a footman, had not leapt into the water, and lift up his head, which was fast in the clay, he had been drowned: but God of his goodness preserved him."

Hall's Chronicle, p. 697.

Sometimes the strangest and funniest stories from history are actually true!

ALAN WYBROW.

Alan Wybrow

Alan Wybrow is a graduate of the Connecticut Institute, USA obtaining a diploma in Children's Literature.

His past experience has included writing and illustrating newspaper comic strips and political cartoons for various publications.

He is a published author, writing and illustrating children's storybooks.

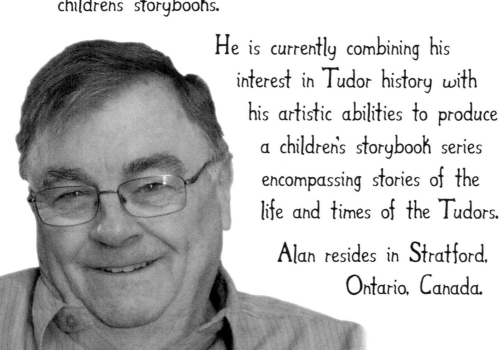

He is currently combining his interest in Tudor history with his artistic abilities to produce a children's storybook series encompassing stories of the life and times of the Tudors.

Alan resides in Stratford, Ontario, Canada.

All About
RICHARD III
Amy Licence

Richard III was a king of England who lived over 500 years ago. He died in battle, and for centuries people thought his bones had been lost. Then, in 2013, he was found buried under a car park in Leicester. The whole world wanted to know about him. Why are so many people interested in his story? Why do some think he was a good king, while others think he was not? What are the mysteries of his life and reign?

Read the facts about Richard III in this book and make up your own mind.

All About
HENRY VII
Amy Licence

Henry VII was the first king of the Tudor dynasty. He spent a lot of his life in exile abroad and no one thought he was important. Then he raised an army and won the Battle of Bosworth and reigned for twenty-four years. He saved money, built some splendid palaces and made the country peaceful after years of war. However, he was not always safe, as plots were made by his enemies to remove him from the throne. How did Henry manage to stay king? Why was his reign so important?

Read the facts about Henry VII in this book and make up your own mind.

MadeGlobal Publishing

Non Fiction History

Jasper Tudor - **Debra Bayani**
Tudor Places of Great Britain - **Claire Ridgway**
Illustrated Kings and Queens of England - **Claire Ridgway**
A History of the English Monarchy - **Gareth Russell**
The Fall of Anne Boleyn - **Claire Ridgway**
George Boleyn: Tudor Poet, Courtier & Diplomat - **Ridgway & Cherry**
The Anne Boleyn Collection - **Claire Ridgway**
The Anne Boleyn Collection II - **Claire Ridgway**
Two Gentleman Poets at the Court of Henry VIII - **Edmond Bapst**
A Mountain Road - **Douglas Weddell Thompson**

"History in a Nutshell Series"

Sweating Sickness in a Nutshell - **Claire Ridgway**
Mary Boleyn in a Nutshell - **Sarah Bryson**
Thomas Cranmer in a Nutshell - **Beth von Staats**
Henry VIII's Health in a Nutshell - **Kyra Kramer**
Catherine Carey in a Nutshell - **Adrienne Dillard**

Historical Fiction

Between Two Kings: A Novel of Anne Boleyn - **Olivia Longueville**
Phoenix Rising - **Hunter S. Jones**
Cor Rotto - **Adrienne Dillard**
The Claimant - **Simon Anderson**
The Truth of the Line - **Melanie V. Taylor**

Children's Books

All about Richard III - **Amy Licence**
All about Henry VII - **Amy Licence**
Tudor Tales William at Hampton Court - **Alan Wybrow**

PLEASE LEAVE A REVIEW

If you enjoyed this book, *please* leave a review at the book seller where you purchased it. There is no better way to thank the author and it really does make a huge difference! *Thank you in advance.*

CPSIA information can be obtained
at www.ICGtesting.com
Printed in the USA
LVOW05s2352121215

466445LV00016B/230/P